Jamaica: The (

Dear Readers:

Thank you for coming this far, inside this book, Jamaica: The Overture of Caribbean Destination Passion & Seduction. I fervently hope that you will go further, by not only getting a copy of this book for yourself, but you will imbibe its contents and tell a friend.

With warm gratitude,

Tyrone

JAMAICA: THE OVERTURE OF CARIBBEAN DESTINATION PASSION & SEDUCTION

TYRONE L. WHITE

Copyright © 2018 Tyrone L. White

All rights reserved.

ISBN-13: 978-1-7919-5949-4

ALL RIGHTS RESERVED. No part of this book may be reproduced or transmitted in any form or by any means, electronic or mechanical, including photocopying, recording, or by any information storage and retrieval system, without permission in writing from the publisher, as any such acts, without written permission from the publisher, constitute unlawful piracy and theft of the author's intellectual property.

DEDICATION

To the indefatigable people who hunt for what is rightfully theirs and the rights of their neighbours, as they keep fighting the good fight, knowing fully well that every battle, in this particular fight, is worth the fight.

CONTENTS

ACKNOWLEDGEMENTS   //X

O JAMAICA   //05

THE STENCH OF THE SUFFRAGE   //08

THE LIFE GONE BY   //12

TOMORROW'S FREEDOM   //14

BONDAGE: THE STRUGGLES CONTINUE   //16

MIGRATION'S THEIR ONLY INTENTION   //19

WHEN VIOLENCE TAKES OVER   //21

THE OTHER SIDE OF GLOAT   //25

FEAR   //28

QUALITY: THE HURTING CONSUMERS' CRY   //30

HUMANITY   //33

THE MAN WITH THE FEARLESS VOICE   //35

NATIONHOOD   //38

THE GHETTOES   //40

IF WE WERE ONLY MEN   //42

BLOODY TIMES   //46

THE BRAVE LONG DEAD   //48

HOMEWARD: JAMAICAN AFAR   //50

THE HARROWING OF JAMAICA   //53

CONQUERING DEATH IN A DREAM   //55

CONTENTS

TIME IS NOT VAIN   //59

FAREWELL   //61

BEFORE WE BECAME ANIMALS   //62

THE KING OF THE SKY   //65

THE COURAGE TO BE STRONG   //67

THE IRONY OF MY GRANDFATHER'S SMILE   //69

MEMORIES OF THE NIGHT   //72

FEELINGS   //74

MARRIAGE PERPETUAL   //76

A PLACE OF SUBLIME PERVERSION   //78

LONELY NO MORE   //81

HOME: THE BECKONING   //83

FROM A DISTANCE   //86

ANCIENT TOGETHERNESS   //88

TEMPTATION   //90

OH, BUT A MAN'S DREAM   //92

REFLECTION   //94

THE PAST   //96

LET ME BE THERE   //98

FORGIVENESS   //101

HAPPINESS FROM A LOVE RESURRECTED   //107

CONTENTS

UNDYING YOUTHFUL LOVE //112

A DREAM OF SUGGESTIVE ADULTERY //114

THE ISLAND OF THE ISLES //116

RESORT //118

OH //120

TWO HEARTS OF EQUAL LOVE //122

RETURN TO THE MOTHERLAND //126

AWAKENED PASSION //129

UNTIMELY LOVE //131

ENJOYING NATURE //134

WHAT CAN I DO? //138

ONLY BUT A COWARD //140

LOYALTY //142

ECSTASY //144

THE BREAK OF SPRING //146

FEARLESS PASSION //147

THE OVERTURE OF CARIBBEAN PASSION //149

FAREWELL TO LOVE //153

MY OWN INFLICTED PAIN //158

A BITTER LOSS //160

HURT //162

CONTENTS

REGRET //164

TREACHERY //166

THE PRICE OF HAPPINESS //168

A HEART INCAPABLE OF LOVE //170

MAKE NEW AGAIN //171

A WEEPING SOUL FOR THE LOVE LOST //173

NOTHING LIKE TRUE LOVE //175

MISERY //177

ACKNOWLEDGMENTS

This book might not have been completed, without the unwavering support of Khalila (my wife) and Khalid, Khalil, and Kolya (my sons). Thanks for allowing me the space and time to carry-out my work. Thanks to all my brothers and sisters for their kindness throughout the time writing this book, especially William and Lorraine for providing me shelter, and to David, Jennifer, and Otist, who never stopped believing in my abilities to work to the end.

Thanks to my aunts "Sister Lee" and "Miss Chin", and to Uncle Fanso, for always providing words of encouragement. Special thanks to Uncle Kenley, for providing printing materials for this book's review.

My gratitude would be incomplete, if I dd not say thank you to all my cousins, who played a part in this book's production, especially to Beverly and Mishelle May, for providing me a typewriter and to Astley for critiquing and always supporting my work, as well as Antoinette and Marie, for being there. Thanks to my very good friends: Quarry, for his words of encouragement and his unwavering belief in me; and Radcliffe, for his support.

And most fundamentally, my heartiest thanks to my parents, Lurline and Phillip, for providing me the guidance to know right and wrong.

Finally, thanks to "Father Guthrie", for his one-liner...his often-used quip: "*You made me smile*".

Jamaica:
The Overture of
Caribbean Destination
Passion & Seduction

PROLOGUE

It does not matter if you are eighteen going on to one hundred and nineteen, you are your own book of poetry with many poems in you, and there is no escaping it. The only trouble being: quite often, poetry is written like an abstract – something out there for other people; not for you; not about you and your realities; when, in fact, poetry is about you and your realities. But, as you will see, Jamaica: The Overture of Caribbean Destination Passion & Seduction captures the essence of these realities to which you can relate.

So, now, forget the belief that poetry is merely romanticism and not for you. Because poetry is for you! For poetry embodies the things...realities...that are a part of the make-up of your daily life: love and hate; sex and unfulfillment; chastity and lust; restraint and hedonism; pain and pleasure; hope and despair; trust and betrayal; rights and injustice; life and murder; beauty and ugliness – all part and parcel of life, which poetry captures; and that is the focus of Jamaica: The Overture of

Caribbean Destination Passion & Seduction.

Jamaica: The Overture of Caribbean Destination Passion & Seduction shows how you dream of love, but you got an overdose of hate; you have a desire for sex, but you are left woefully unfulfilled; you seek pleasure, but you ended up with only intense pain; you look for hope, but all you experience is dark despair; you trust, but you are brutally betrayed...

Only by focussing on concrete human experiences that Jamaica: The Overture of Caribbean Destination Passion & Seduction was able to capture the realities, and put these realities into words that, hopefully, you, dear readers, will appreciate. As you will see, some of these poems encapsulate certain themes where politics and morals are in disharmony to the degree that the people suffer; where pleasure, love, and human satisfaction are priced in blood, sweat, and tears. But, nonetheless, Jamaica, for all its ills, throughout its hills and vales, you will find passion; and you will be seduced by it.

This being so, it is the author's hope that you will be captivated by the allure of Jamaica: The Overture of Caribbean Destination Passion &

Seduction. As such, you will close your eyes, breathe the fresh breath of life, and bask in the undeniable realism of a time long gone, yet ever-present in your daily yearnings...a time when you sit beneath the shades of your porch and feed to satiety on nature's beauty. Who knows, you might just reach out and touch! But, it is, also, OK, if you become a little incensed with the actions of those whose sole intent is to destroy the thing of beauty that you hold dear.

In all if this, whether it is at a time when the night is departing, or when the day is at its fullest, or when the evening is drawing near, hopefully, you will still be filled with a heightened sense of wanting to read the next poem, even if you are finding it difficult to leave the one that you are reading, at the present time – written with a smile.

O JAMAICA

Sorrowful am I, for my people
All have gone astray.
Lived we once, peaceful and simple;
Filled with laughter and gay;

But godlike men, we know not were snide,
With heavenly promises they allure
So, we sacrifice all, even our pride,
In order to ensure

That victory is theirs,
As we play their inimical game.
O, many suffered…myriads shed tears;
For life we show great disdain.

So, our neighbours we murder…

Pervasion of atrocities we gained fame.
O, our country plagued by wanton disorder,
Nought is our honour, dignity, and shame.

Is there no God in the sanctuary?
Peradventure, His ecclesiastics have gone
 astray.
Their hands, too, have become sanguinary;
For our lamentations, there is none to pray.

Yeah, none amongst them for us our battles to
 fight
Nay, none amongst them for us will be strong;
So, it is for us to do what is right
And bring an end to all that is wrong.

For it is the fulness of time
To regain our pride and sacrifice self no longer;
So we make our collective purposes shine
As together we are stronger

To stand up to them all,
Even though they wield great power
To their enticements, we will ne'er again crawl
And from their reign of terror, we no longer
 cower.

So, our battered loins we gird

To take us out of the mire;
Championed our voiceless voices to be heard;
'Tis folly to wait for a messiah.

Yeah, let us lend our strength to rewriting our
   history
Albeit, we'll forget not our past.
United we'll stand in victory
Beneath our fluttering on the mast.

THE STENCH OF THE SUFFRAGE

To them we'll not go
For we accordingly know
'Tis that time again
When truth and honour they feign
That the past we repeat
Though ourselves we defeat

By executing the ungodly act
When they we enact
As servants of the authoritative chairs
In the palace of nation's affairs.
Alas, servants become pompous and hallowed
And into the filthy mire masters wallowed.

We see and know them all
Thus, in their clutches we will not fall,

As our trusting ancestors before,
Whom they did assure
That from the power of their word
Their voices would always be heard

Not knowing that it was merely an empty
    pledge
To precipitate them over the political edge
Long before they did realise
That their aim is to covertly tribalise
The inhabitants and their noble political worth
In this the land of our birth

But we will not err again the same
For, at last, we fathom the rules of their game:
Hatred and hostility, amongst us, they nurture
Though their faces overt a picture of virtue.
Lambs they be, with the venom of a snake
Cuddle them and we pay dearly for such a
    mistake.

So thanks to the gods, for sure,
They cannot fool us anymore
When their words of persuasion we hear
We, at once, see the inauspicious sign: beware
And immediately, our anger they provoke
We sigh in contemplation: on their lying words
    they would choke

For pithy; in their toploftiness, they do not
   know
That the hem of their slips will always show
The nastiness of their venal political systems
Into which they themselves may yet become
   victims
It could happen to them, one of these days
Then, predators will be reduced to the preys

And, if this, by chance, becomes true
No harm to them, we would do
Preserving their rights, as citizens, would be
   the aim
Even though, retributions for their wrongs, we
   would claim
But for the sake of justice, they would be tried
And by the final outcome we would verily
   abide

Albeit, it would be our fervent hope
That they would not profit from the end of a
   rope
Yeah, indubitably, we oppose and abhor
   murder
So we would find no favour in their alar arms
   from the girder
Nonetheless, from their Janus-faced politics, let
   us be

For it is high time that they open their eyes to see

That we discern things better than most
So, we ne'er again will host
Their parasitic intentions
Characteristic of contemporary conventions,
Where they ardently promulgate democracy
While they but be drunken by their own hypocrisy.

For, as their lips they open
A thousand words are spoken
But none will bear fruit
They are only intent on a great loot:
To completely and utterly annex your heart and your soul
By the words to cajole.

THE LIFE GONE BY

Behold, those memories come flooding home
From their far away land;
They are coming in torrents, on their own
To take me by the hand

For a journey down the rocky road
Of the unforgettable life gone by.
Oh, I deemed to accept this as the mode
For old sentimental fools like me to cry.

So, mindless am I, of the tidal tears,
Smoothly outpouring from my eyes.
They are fettered emotions gleaned from the
    harsh juvenile years,
Which make me now realise:

Mounting the slope of success is not as difficult
   as it seems,
Though doing so solitarily requires sedulous
   efforts always.
For, now, the great realities of my dreams
Fulfilled I; profuse comforting joy for the rest
   of my days.

TOMORROW'S FREEDOM

Prosecutor's world
I find myself
Prosecutor's world

Behold I, His Majesty
And his eyes hold a wanton jeer
Focus on the jury
Yeah, my being is seized by fear
Wander my eyes for my barrister
He cannot be found
The feeling is bitter
To hell my fate is bound.

Prosecutor's world
I find myself
Prosecutor's world

O, the filth of the system is palpable…
Justice there is none.
They said I am culpable
For deeds have I ne'er done.
O rights, what meagre pittance for the common citizenry!
But, for the elite, greatly enshrined.
The land's perpetually saturated with draconian misery
Where the quick and the dead are politically aligned.

Prosecutor's world
I find myself
Prosecutor's world

By dawn next, they will hang me
Nay, I may not till the morrow survive.
Yeah, the sunshine I still can see
Woe, knowing I won't be alive.
Howbeit, even moribund, dedication I give…
The principles of my people I shall not betray.
For as long as fellow martyrs live
The movement towards liberty will stay.

Prosecutor's world
I find myself
Prosecutor's world

BONDAGE: THE STRUGGLES CONTINUE

Toilers of this field we have been for so very, very long
Ne'er have we done anything wrong.
Nurtured we are in the field of servitude;
Deeply instilled with the highest esteem of subjective attitude.

Humbly we bend our backs every day
Under our nithings' whip and masters' sway
O, if but a moment's respite from our toil we take
Grave are the consequences of such a trivial mistake.

Wretched children we are: owing obedience

they say;
Thus, from us they extract and exact the things
    they may.
They defile our women...rape our land
Commanded they, these things we be civilized
    enough to understand

As elements of the complex process of our
    transition,
Relative to the definitive interest of our
    education
In the continuous construction of a nation
    new...
In a country that pleases only the few...

Where there are several manifestations of the
    flaws
In the capricious and wicked nature of the laws
That hold sway based on the might
Of the few who determine the right

In accordance with their inner sanctum of ends
Where only the interests of friends
They stoutly and unwaveringly defend
Hypocritically, and...shamelessly, to the end.

And if the courage, we find, to complain,
It is always, all in vain

For they merely make a another promulgation
To authoritatively silence the voice of agitation.

O, our dear people before
Have faced this barbarity for sure
Nay, their sacred spirits will find no peace
'Till the shackles of our existence they release

'Till the world offers a listening ear to our cries
Or the arsenal for destruction we realise…
Alas, devoid of…we be… we merely wait
Not that we are resigned to seeming fate.

Natheless, awhile, home we go, as a bloodline proud
Home to dream of the day, when the abeng will be loud
For as long as God's presence with us abide
Inevitably, we will stand at victory's side.

MIGRATION'S THEIR ONLY INTENTION

Behold, our seeds,
As they take flight,
From a country plagued with dire needs
And devastatingly chronic plight.
Yeah, there is a mighty rush
For the great light
Where the grass is lush
And the future is bright.

Day by day, they are scattered and sowed–
Not omitting a single grain.
They spring from all sides of the road,
With one common aim:
Induce they those mighty diplomats to believe
Their words as worthy and pure

Thus, the endorsement of permissible leave
Seek they for another shore.

O, some succeed
Others fall mercilessly by the way.
Not to say they will sit and bleed
And try not another day.
For they are crafty and strong;
They simply know no fall.
Whether unpatriotic, unscrupulous, or
    principally wrong
Yonder land they must go, one and all.

.

WHEN VIOLENCE TAKES OVER

Behold, a great many times they have tried
O, many have suffered, and many have died;
But a people they are of lofty pride.

So, with solemn dignity they set
On a militant ride to the grounds: not for the wet.
The enemies they met

Like the other times before
Only this time they are sure
After this, nay, they battle no more.

For determined are they to trample the formidable gate
And wantonly annihilate

The ones they mercilessly hate.

Yeah, the ones who filled their lives with turmoil
Must be rid from their soil
To live the reign of peace for the never ending while.

Now, the bloody battle starts
O, there are the hurts and pains of many hearts
As warriors' bodies are brutally dismantled in parts.

By God, such a sickening sight…even vultures could not bear
The noxious smell of death everywhere
And, the earth, with human and animal blood did smear.

For the victors, 'twas a saga of bloody gain
While it is a great shame
That defeats always remain

Yeah, a tearful…hurting…humiliating disgrace
A bitter and shameful loss of face
To always become victims…fallen to the defeat of such a race.

Howbeit, pray, do not harbour the unintended
For with gallantry and fortitude they have
   defended
Their ideals, 'till the battle ended.

Thereupon, being weak and unfed
With daunting days ahead
They retreated from the place of the dead.

Their dead they not bury
Their wounded they not carry
For they aspire to find sanctuary.

Thus, to the mountains they go
Albeit, progress is slow
Nevertheless, they accordingly know

That with them the enemies wroth and vex
Filled with desires to terminate…even to
   merely perplex
Their aspiration of securing the apex

Of their ancestors' dreams
Of repossessing the land of their genes
That was subjugated by forceful means.

But, once again, the grueling price they have
   paid

For the expected victory has been delayed
Hence, unto them heroic welcome won't bade.

O, if only the gods have shown more favour
They would have lost never
They would have rid the enemies from their
    land forever

Nonetheless, they dream of another
    time…another call
Then, they won't fall;
Defeat will be crushed, and victory stands tall.

THE OTHER SIDE OF GLOAT

When our tables are abundantly laden,
And we have a richly endowed garden
When the tempest is roaring
And the tears of humanity are pouring,
Those are the times we should be a friend
And a helping hand is what we should lend

Today, our horizon with sunshine is gloriously bright
Resplendent in our habiliment of silk delight
And dazzling in the lime light.
Building castles to show our might
For us and ours alone
Without a glancing thought of happiness, but for our own

Alas, what little do we know
About the forgotten seeds we did sow
In the winds of time far behind
For fertile grounds some did find
And their fruits have shown
Into the greatness they have grown

So, we should make no mistake
Those are the very fruits from the basket of life
   we will partake
Then, wherefore
We trample on the poor
We corral them in paddocks that are
   unpropitious
We, egad, and punish them for their seeming
   failures to be ambitious

When it is our duties to mankind, we abdicate
Yet, the temerity to ascribe to ourselves today's
   leaders great
It is high time that we show some care
And withal to be acutely aware
Of the things lying in-wait ahead
For tomorrow we will be led

By the toilsome beings baseborn
Those whom we chastised and treated with
   scorn.

Wherewith, shall we longer boast
When the morrow's great feast, they will host
Filled with splendor, oh, so divine
Principalities begging bread; lords of the
    manors yearning to dine

FEAR

I have broken the line…divagated…strayed
Corruption and wickedness have seized my ways.
Upon the innocent I have preyed –
Cut short the length of their days.

Alas, the moment of trial is here
And…o…I am at the end of the iniquitous road.
Who, for me, will care?
Who is going to neighbour me with this load?

Among men doeth I know there is none
For it is my sole duty…the act of truth…
To requite the wrongs that I have done
Throughout the journey of my days of youth.

Nevertheless, thou patient one, for my sins, do
    not me despise
Do not drive me away from thy fold
Do not, from this accursed creature, turn away
    thy compassionate eyes
Do not block my path to thy kingdom behold

Yeah, from thy kingdom deny me not ingress
Hide not thy smile of clemency from me, I
    humbly pray;
But with morals…rectitude…benevolence thou
    me bless
And, with thy rod of wisdom, thou shepherds
    me along the holy way

To humility, justice, peace, and love;
So, become I my brother's trust and loyal
    servant, in their time of lamentations and
    needs,
Just like a divine attendant from above
Who is always doing graciously noble deeds.

QUALITY: THE HURTING CONSUMERS' CRY

There are these two athletes, with speed of
 horror;
And, throughout our land, they are filled with
 fame.
To thousands of hearts, they wrought heavy
 sorrow;
So, with them, people inclined not to play even
 a single game.

Howbeit, their prices stupendous are; yea very
 dear:
For in the sprints they are amazingly piercing
 and lightning fast;
But mindful of how their stamina are stretched
 with care,

Their demise is o'er the distance where they
   ne'er last.

Sustain they not the courses' length...
Satisfying our consuming purposes defined.
O, such supernatural speed, with a pittance of
   strength
Comprehensively petrifies the human mind.

Thus, we'd like their governors, and people in
   high places
To inject remedial medicines in their situation;
Hence, become they more congenial for all
   races
Bringing satiated pride to us as a nation.

Making the value of the money on them we
   spend
Reflect in the satisfaction and enjoyment we
   obtain
These are the things we defend...
We sincerely seek no other gain.

We want about these weaklings something be
   done
For the ways they dissatisfy us are
   unforgivable sins.
The consuming public finds this to be no joke,

or fun,
When the contents of our purchases wantonly
    effuse from their tins.

So, demand us succulent products to reign in
    different consumption games...
Sporting their thick enrichment, with pride,
    like kings, resplendent in robes of silk.
Thereupon we will shout: "Betnay and
    Nestnay, long live your mellow names.
No more are you the weak, half-sweetened
    condensed milk"

HUMANITY

Look, they are wretched, dirty, and miserably poor!
Their pathetically nauseating looks dampen the eyes, move the stomach, and disturb the mind.
They have nothing to live for anymore
Hence, in their squalid conditions they resigned.

The filthy corners of the streets have they made their own;
O, with them, everyone eschews the thoughts of any dealings.
Possess they not the measliest comfort of a home;
But, ah, they do have feelings!

For they swelter in the heat; shudder in the
 rain
Feel the brutal hurt; o, they sadly cry.
What senseless loquacity that they are insane;
For they embrace life, like you and I!

Yeah, they are but sorrowful preys of the harsh
 realities of a brutal fate;
Thereby, it is for us... oh nobles, oh, survivors
 of the time
To concordantly unlock that restorative gate;
Enabling them to savour the joy of the
 magnificent sunshine.

Pray, do not blame their down-fall on systems,
 nor rulers, nor deeds.
For we are fleas of one coat, scattered
 throughout the fields of these soils;
Nay, we should no longer thus oblivious be of
 their needs
Instead, let us share with them the best of our
 spoils.

THE MAN WITH THE FEARLESS VOICE

It is the days of trials and severe privation, and
 he's become an illustrious fighter
Who unconditionally knows no hurt, no pain,
 no fear…
Oh, mindful of how the battles intensify…how
 the situations get tighter…
His opponents are never able to jab him into
 the submissive ropes from which himself he
 couldn't clear.

Here is a man of wisdom; and a paramount
 part he played
In the difficult and costly brewing of a new
 wine,
So that the tables can be richly laid

Not for clouts alone to dine

But rather justice, peace, and meaningful
 existence for all
In this the land of our birth.
Thus, myriads of us, proles, answered his call,
With vivacious breath of fertility in the
 enhancement of our self-worth.

On the dawn of regular days, he starts the
 never-ending hare...
Challenging the citizenry to join the forum.
Oh, how his knowledge and teachings on
 issues of burning importance flare
Not with the pomposity of men vain, but with
 kindness of heart, great understanding,
 moderation and decorum.

In his profound intellectual voice, he invokes
 that we not be frustrated in our fights
For the demolition of injudicious systems
Thereby, fulfilling our rights
To no longer be fettered victims

Alas, detractors have used propaganda and
 other sensationalized facts
To colour him as trumpery, apocryphal –
 relishing the surripio path of glorious fame.

But the faithful followers we be acknowledged
 such astoundingly remarkable acts
As pure and undefiled...purely in the interest
 of our country's gain.

And, so, we came! We came like wild fire
At the height of the dry seasons.
We all gathered to listen...gathered to
 vehemently admire
The man with the courageous voice...the man
 who's fearless voice flavoured our lives with
 purposeful reasons.

NATIONHOOD

My life of turpitude has come to an end,
As I leave the world of turmoil.
Atrocities no more I will defend
Neither will I again bespatter man's blood on
 the soil.

From generation to generation, thousands have
 been slain
But none were valiant enough to stop this
 damn feud.
Bah, there is justifiably no gain
O, only ourselves we delude.

So, the stream of blood must cease its flow
And the anachronistic hatchet goes beneath the
 earth

The land be fattened, and an amicable seed
  grow
Into a blood line of unity, magnitude, and
  noble worth.

For not by might we obtain sanity
Nor by blood we find wisdom.
But through morals and dignity
We seek gaining the kingdom.

Tyrone L. White

THE GHETTOES

O, ye inimical neighbours,
Take heed.
Anarchy in its spate
There is a nation seized by fright...
O, the cries of oppression everywhere
A lamenting people in need,
No leadership to be found
For an inhabitant in sorrowful plight.

A country with a dearth of care...
Heaping live coal on its own head;
The inferno brightens the horizon
Yet unable they to see the flame;
For the beauties of its cities
Are pictured within the spectre of the living
    dead.

Nay!
No one will shoulder the blame.

For everyone's become saturated
Within his own selfish greed;
Without the pittance of care for wretched
    shadows
Beyond their garden wall.
O, there is simply no compunction
For the life they lead:
Insatiably uplifting themselves,
While others mercilessly fall.

But...ah...ardently adjure I,
Take heed
My ignoble neighbours
Take heed
Hence, we lie like wounded hogs...
And from gaping holes we bleed
From the vicious sword's
Piercing edge that we breed.

IF WE WERE ONLY MEN

We, the plebeians of our country, cannot find
 simple peace or rest....
Daily we are being devastated and oppressed
By honourably sovereign men and think tanks
 of the day
Who demand that we be obsequious to
 everything they say.

For they wield infinite power and legislative
 control...
Arrogantly perpetrating our daily role
As alienated citizens in the land of our birth
Where the fruits ne'er mirrored our arduous
 labour's worth...

Where our meagre and barren tuppence

Embed us in mere subsistence.
Alas, from pittance, loathsome as these,
Our pouches they reave for their high fees

To augment their protuberant treasury…
Disposing on our people severe torment and draconic misery,
By keeping us under conditions that could scarcely be more austere
While their bulging bellies reveal the enriching of their own welfare

In this cancerous syndrome of life, our champions' militant voices are never heard;
For their cries are drowned in the power of the mighty men's word
And if this we merely criticise
We court the unequivocality of our demise.

Moreover, their self-orchestrated system of justice and equity, we dare not impugn
Howbeit, from the powers of these, they are immune.
They are unencumbered in their continuous mutilation of our nation
Void of any act of expiation

Nevertheless, many amongst us betray unto

them tremendously great veneration…
Sacrificing our children's future, as an oblation…
Burnishing them with ardent praise
As to the heights of gods they did raise.

What history we write, I not know;
See the harsh and degenerating conditions of our existence, as they will always show
The flaws and blunders of the authoritative range
Which, unquestionably, warrants a comprehensively fundamental change

To a system offering the populace a more favourable chance.
Thus, like our noble counterparts, our lives we enhance
For the security of our children's rights
So that they will not suffer, as we have, the same plights.

Instead our children's future road will be great
And for that walk they will not have to wait
So up, with a smile of hope on their journey they will go
And along the fertile paths, the seeds of success they will sow

But, lo, our children's journey to success
 continued to be delayed
And in utter hopelessness they stayed
For we are not man enough to stand up and
 fight
To secure our children's most basic right

We blatantly ignore our children's wild
 screams
And obligingly provide fodder for their elusive
 dreams
So that they are inhibited from securing the
 things they seek
Because we are spineless, insipid, and weak.

For if we were only men
The things we would have done differently,
 then
Control of our country, we would have taken
 back
And never again, allow our self-worth to come
 under attack.

BLOODY TIMES

'Tis the everlasting days of severe violence
'Tis the eon of eons of despicable crimes.
Listen to the living dead-silence
As the faceless clock mercilessly chimes

Heralding the end...
Another life is lost.
Whether kin, a stranger, a foe or a friend
Insulting is the cost

Of human life, o, so cheap
So, death becomes commonplace.
O, ruth, for the poor souls no one will weep...
Just another carnage of our race.

Will the vendetta see no end?
O, vanquished are we
Burnt bridges cannot mend
When men are not free.

So, the guns incessantly blaze...
The barbarous life takes roots.
Filled with threnody are the days
When saints enfold the depravity of brutes.

THE BRAVE LONG DEAD

In the days of indomitable strength, laughter to
 many lips...gladsomeness of myriads of
 hearts he's brought...
In his quest for equity, love, and harmony the
 impossible he's wrought.

Without the looming shadow of a thought of
 fattening his coffer, or any other gain,
Deeds of chivalry and patriotism executed he,
 through the cyclone, the sunshine, and the
 rain.

Yeah, through the traverse of time, shown he
 great valour
Preserving the apothegm of his people:
 "A warrior's life should be pure of

dishonour."

Alas, no vision has he of the agony, emptiness,
    loneliness, desiderata of his winter days.
For the zeal of youth – the vivacity of spirit –
    saw the river of strength flowing always.

But, o, now he's died a wicked death, with no
    one to write his obituary.
The wind heareth his cry; the sun wipes the
    brine from his face and the earth's become is
    only sanctuary

HOMEWARD: JAMAICAN AFAR

'Tis the season of festive mood
So, the tables are richly laid.
Alas, greatly I brood
O'er mistakes I have made.

Many, many years ago,
When life was in its spring,
Oh, progress was slow
And I felt the sting

Of the venomous snake:
Hardship, poverty, and cold.
So, my land I did forsake
Vowed ne'er again to behold.

I set sail
To dwell among another race
Oh, from my heart came much gale
When landed I, at this place.

Land of the free and fair
'Twas freedom at last;
Essence of prosperity in the air
So, I gave up the past.

And started I, my life anew
Fervently hoping that someday I would be
   great.
Thus, with sedulity and fortitude, the things I
   would do
To abide in the realm of a magnate.

But, now, my life with nostalgia and longing
   agitate
And there be no peace of mind
For to the indomitable fate
I am zealously inclined

To earnestly start
A rekindling of the stirring fire
And rid my aching heart
Of its homesick desire.

So, here I come again;
Here I return!
For thee to mollify the pain
And make mild the burn.

THE HARROWING OF JAMAICA

It is the seventeenth one she's got
One man per brat.
O, the certitude of life getting harder
Another child without a father…

Another child to share the one-room tenement
Alas, mother is six months adrift with the rent.
Ruth, the space is piteous for its rest
So, it fights the grab and sleeps on mother's
    available breast.

Will this one be different from the previous?
Nostrils draining filthy mucous!
Its spring of life has no memories to cherish
But, by God's help, it will not perish.

So, like the others before, it will survive:
From the family pot, it will be kept alive.
Devoid of preparation that's life's road;
Poverty and suffering are the generations' goad.

O, what will it be when older it grows?
The morrow's dispensation no one knows.
But, the hardship of life, it will embrace
The sombre companion of its race.

Memories of the harsh birth approaches demise
O, when will they be wise?
From afar, one can see the profusion…
A shadow of the incessant confusion.

For it will be the eighteenth one
Alas, for another man.
O, the certitude of life getting harder
Another child without a father.

CONQUERING DEATH IN A DREAM

Behold, my health is failing
My body is ailing.
Albeit, I have no wealth...no power
Give me ink and paper to draft I the testament
   of my final hour.

For imprisoned I am, in my own home
Lying here, all alone, with my eyes the ceiling
   to rome
Like a paralytic confined to his squalid bed
Awaiting I am to be dead

O, there's just no hope for me any more
Time has aggregated my score.
As the light goes from mauve to grey to black

Knoweth I, my life's coming under attack.

Indeed, the final rites are about to take place
My past, present, and future mock to my face.
Though I possess my mental receptacles still,
With thoughts rational and confusion spill

From my eddying head by the clout of a mace
I'd rather be deracinated from this race.
Yea, I'd take pleasure in witnessing the elegy of
   my turn
To pay respect to the land where evildoers
   burn

Than behold my spirit and mind in anguish
My body and soul languish
Yeah, my evanescent body being lamented
And my broken being incessantly tormented

By the prowling preys of rapine souls
And my flesh predatorily ravished by vermin
   and ghouls
Who have this sickening… pathetic… delight
For one's misery, suffering…martyrdom…and
   plight.

O, what pains in the final moments to bear
Overwhelmingly so, when there's no one to

care;
Nay, no beloved to hold me, kiss me, and weep
As drift off I to the land of the deep

Where, in the life of another sphere,
The destiny of my days began to be made clear:
I saw a giant, his back twain mountains faced
And, at his feet, the deadliest beasts of the earth abased.

Though there were legions of adversaries him around
The giant without effort found
Otherworldly strengths abound
To simply withstand his ground

Ready to crush his enemies like a simple worm mound
While the cowering enemies made nary a sound
Yeah, a single word whispered none dare
Instead swelter they in fear

Of his majestic sword's blade
And his colossus shadow's shade,
Which shows all the plans they have made
To be a colossal mistake, as with celerity away

they did fade.

Enquired I, about me, after this man's powers and might
Lo, my spirits were lifted to the preternatural height.
For I was told I was walking in the land that shall come to pass
And I was looking at myself in the reflective glass

Then, with nay warning, from o'er yonder mountainside
I heard a voice from a long, rumbling brontide:
"In this land, thou cannot stay;
Arise, now, from thy slumber, and be on thy way."

Thence, I realised I was only dreaming...
Notwithstanding the true meaning:
Though my body and soul may be at strife
I shall always conquer death with life.

Time Is Not Vain

Hark, time's going by;
So, don't delay
Pray, hie
Or ye'll pay.

Say ye weren't told
Then ye lied.
Only thyself, in time, to scold
Thus, I beseech thee don't abide.

As the clock ticks away
Time becomes a chronological waste
Hence, tarry not another day
Yea! Adjure I, make haste.

Oh, the resplendent light shines now

Verily, time gone never comes again.
Thus, to dilatory habits never bow;
Never treat time as vain.

FAREWELL

Ye must be brave
Don't weaken and cry.
When standeth thou at my grave
Ye must be brave
Oh, thy strength thou save
To relive my memories, by and by.
Ye must be brave
Don't weaken and cry.
For my spirit, thee I gave
Thus, we'll meet in the sky.
Ye must be brave
Don't weaken and cry.

BEFORE WE BECAME ANIMALS

There lived an old man and his ageing wife
Have they no children of their own.
But throughout their everyday life
The old couple never feels alone.

In the mornings, she feeds the big laying hen
While he attends to the squealers in the pen
And, then, cheerily their basket's laden,
With the blessings from their garden.

As the morning passed away,
Gaily, 'round the yard they go;
Then, for a few hours of the day
With their mattocks, they till, they fallow, and
    they sow.

Thence from work themselves they divest
For the old mango tree's shelter
Where their old bones they rest
From the sun's swelter.

After the tiredness of their bodies, they ease
They indulge themselves in a few bites
Of plantain, bread, and cheese –
More than enough, they say, to satisfy their
 delicate appetites.

Humble folk they be
By the simple life they live.
But happiness in people they always want to
 see
So, from the little they have, much they freely
 give.

Thus, when evenings come, they stand at their
 gate,
With a decorated basket in one hand,
Patiently, for the destitutes they wait,
To gladly share the fat of the land.

Thereafter, when they themselves are fed
They'd laugh, they'd sing, and they'd pray.
Those are the delicate things they would do,
 before going to bed

To wholly regain their strength, for the coming day.

THE KING OF THE SKY

Sitteth I, in the glare of the glorious Jamaican
    e'en sun,
Watching another day of nature's wonder goes
    by.
Oh, what bliss…what fun
Beholding his majesty on his throne on high.

He rises zingy in the east
Not missing a single day,
Emitting precious light to man, plant and beast
Along his kingly way.

He is a dedicated and diligent being…
One who's always there;
Though, sometimes, he cannot be seen
And, other times, he does disappear,

He is not gone; he is just soothing beneath the
   cloud
From the sweltering heat and balmy rain.
So be assured, he will soon remove his shroud
To continue his majestic reign:

Of marvelous works of wonder
Which has zenith but no end.
Thence to wax o'er yonder
To brighten the life of an unknown friend

THE COURAGE TO BE STRONG

We are sailing on a smooth ocean
We are drifting on a wave-less sea
We are gliding in slow motion
We are overwhelmed with glee.

There are no encumbrances in our way
There are no mountains to climb
As we progress from day to day
Everything is very, very fine.

Life is, oh, so divine
Life is, indeed, kind
We are feeling most sublime
There is a joyous peace of mind.

Nothing can harm us anymore

Nothing can ever go wrong
Our people have gotten the cure:
It is the courage to be strong

THE IRONY OF MY GRANDFATHER'S SMILE

My grand-father never laughs
He only smiles.
When he does, it wafts
For many, many miles.

Amazing his smile may be
It doesn't light up the place
What you will see
Are those massive wrinkles on his face

Entwine with many perfect views
Of golden…char-coal blotted…teet'
Man! The funny things my grand-father exudes
Thrillingly pulsate the most quiescent

heartbeat:

He suds and drains at the mouth
Amid humorous utterances in a drawl
He lingeringly groans and gruffly shouts
Like an unruly hog in a kraal.

As he rumbustiously rumbles on…
Giving it all he has got…
You wish you were gone
From such an uproarious spot

For you, yourself, cannot help laughing
At the grotesque sight before you.
Yea! You join in the wallow and free fling
Like under the powers of a strong brew.

Alas, not for long
The life of this ridiculous spree
As my grand-father's voice, oh, so strong
Abruptly solemnises the moment's glee.

In his antiquated manner, he would scold…
Displaying a sallow like gaze:
"No respect you, younger generation, have for the old.
It is time we eccentrics purge you of your grinning ways."

And, so, this absurd scene would be over
My grand-father belches in style
Gets laughingly sober
And said, "You made me smile!"

MEMORIES OF THE NIGHT

Behold, the sun is asleep,
My love
Let's take a romantic walk…
Lost in the beauties of the heavens above.

Likened unto waltzing clouds,
Let's glide through nature's bliss
Let's lingeringly burn each other
In a fiery kiss.

Oh, the sumptuous moon waxes in beauty…
Emitting its seductive light.
Let's intensify our passion of soul fire –
The wild storm of love through the night.

So that when the night is rested

And the morn breaks bright and clear
Cherished and treasured will be the beauties
Of the precious memories we'll always share.

FEELINGS

Behold, my love,
in the chill of the early moon,
I beseech thee,
come 'round
to rekindle
sparks
of soul fire
abound.

To intoxicate
my unquenched being
with the light and delicate wine
of thy lips,
while
leisurely caress I
thy locks

with my fingertips.

Oh,
enfold me,
squeeze me
extremely tight,
amidst the sound of
soft
whispering music…
the feeling of tender pain…
the rich glow
of candle light.

Yes,
my beloved,
surrender unto me
unashamedly
effusively
the place of thy fire
so that I can
passionately
ravenously
ravish the suggestive fruit
of my heart's desire.

MARRIAGE PERPETUAL

Oh, enamoured are thine eyes
For thy love, I suffer men's despise.

But ours is a love of twain souls that assuredly combine
The spirituality of beings divine

Forever, I will unabashedly abide
At the comfort of thy side.

So gently take my hand
As your dearly beloved husband

And for the journey of this life,
You'll be my diuturnal wife.

Ne'er will you taste ache of the heart
Ne'er will we be apart.

And even in the land of the deep,
Where we take our perpetual sleep,

Our ardent fire shall continue to burn
Yielding warmth in the comfort of our urn.

A PLACE OF SUBLIME PERVERSION

Welcome to the "**Sacred Paphian-Love Theatre**",
Where the charming voice of seductive passion sings;
Come now, pray, not later
For this is a night fit for lords, masters, and kings.

So, filled with grace and charm
They come sauntering in pairs,
And, on the crook of an arm,
A sparkling beauty each man bears.

With euphony in the air
Some take the dance floor
While others stand fully aware

Of a different passion soon to be exuded
   galore.

Now, the curtain raiser has ended
And the real performances are about to start.
I hope you won't be offended
By what I am about to impart.

In caliginous corners of room wonderland
Carnal swords, sumptuous labial, sultry
   tongues…wax and grow
Like passion and music swathing hand in hand
To the tune of moans and groans, chorusing in
   wanton glow.

Oh, like virulent stormy days
The sensuous battles intensified.
They rapturously pounced upon their preys
Without shame, without dignity…without
   pride

And when the final cadence is song; the curtain
   is brought low
The gratified audience paid homage.
Thereupon, it's time to go,
Or chance tarnishing their image.

Home they go, like men of nobility…

And the virtuous ladies they would like to be.
But ah, if others only know the reality
Of their faithful's recent spree

There'd emerge dark belligerent pictures,
With very painful repercussions.
Not only would there be serious curtain
    lectures
But tearful moments of very shameful
    separations.

LONELY NO MORE

Oh, I remember, 'twasn't the autumn gone;
'Twasn't the summer before.
'Twas the season when a fresh flower of spring
  was born
Thenceforth, my winters aren't the same any
  more.

The wretched, lonely…desolate…life came to
  its end…
Gusted away, leaving nary a dust speck of, at
  last.
For unto me, a plebeian, the gods did send
A royal gift to rid me of that confounding past.

A gift the pith of purity…so divine…
Not of the daughters of the earth.

Oh, the bliss…the joy…of being mine
Gave life to my stolid life; now, a wondrous
    birth.

The birth of warm and tender togetherness
From thence and forever, always.
Intertwining two souls of celestial love and
    spiritual happiness
For the joyous journey of our days.

HOME: THE BECKONING

My love,
My beloved,
I am going.
I must be gone,
I cannot stay.
Linger I not another day.

Oh, my beloved,
My love,
There is so much tenderness in thy love
So much warmth from thy being
And
Passion
Fire
In my desire to be with thee.
But, no!

I cannot stay
I must be on my way.

It might be years from now,
My beloved,
My love,
Before return I to thee.
But, sorrowfully,
To erstwhile vows,
Where no happiness allows,
I must go
I cannot stay
I cannot delay.

But my love,
My beloved
When I go
Even the gods
Cannot keep us apart.
So
I'll return,
For thee to quench the burn
I'll come again,
So that with thee, I will remain
For, my love,
My beloved,
Like the blue mahoe tall
True love shadows all

True love never downward cast
But
Celestially, stands proud
It's never under another's shroud
It never answers another's call
So
From, thee, afar,
I'll ne'er again abide
Perpetually, I'll be, by thy side

FROM A DISTANCE

The sound of my distant drum
Beats in my ears.
Tender and passionate are the sounds
Coming from the one who cares.

Oh, thou art all the company I have
During the dreary hours of the day.
Thou art comfort and warmth
When in my cold and lonely bed I lay.

Oh, my distant drum
Thy intimacy is so fervent, so strong
Thou warmth my heart with melody
Lifting my spirit all day long.

Yeah, sweet…beloved…distant drum
Thy servant hears thy beat loud and clear.
Though far thou art
To me thou art always near.

ANCIENT TOGETHERNESS

Oh, beloved, thou art mine
And I am thine.

Until we are perpetually apart
The chasings of this heavenly fervour will not thwart.

We will revive the memories of yesterday
No obstacles can stand in our way.

We will waltz through the motions of the morrow
Our hearts will know no sorrow.

We will share the blessings the gods have sent
For the journey of this life is lent.

All our days will be likened to a fresh flower
Joyously spent will be every hour.

But if we be touched by a despondent mood
With tender loving words we will soothe.

On the shoulders of the other we will lean
A source of strength to our being.

And come the passage of our days of old
We will revel in the land of gold.

TEMPTATION

Behold, the lascivious serpent
Hissing through my garden
Assaying to beguile my beloved wife.
Not, during my mortuary days, even
Will it ever be able to perplex and wreck my life.

Using the glib from his hissing tongue
In the conviction of my love
That she will not end up dead
If she with him
Will connive to go to bed.

But my love is aware
That in the cool of the evening
I will come 'round

And any change in the climate of our existence
The evidence will be found.

Forsooth, my beloved knows
Drinking of the wine of adultery
Breached the hallowed engraved in stones
Hence life giveth to the flaming swords
Where banishment perpetual beyond still
 bones.

So, take heed
Ye lustful and illicit dragon
Take heed and go thy way…
Go fill thy carnal thirst from thine own stream
And into thine own garden have thy prurient
 play.

OH, BUT A MAN'S DREAM

Nay! She is not my wife.
But she is, verily, my dearly beloved bride.
Oh, she is the perpetual passion of my life…
The ray which warms my heart with pride.

Though our marriage is in its Anno Domini,
The feeling's like we 'ere wed only moments
    ago.
Time stilled; it ne'er goes by;
The gaily spirit of her love has never been low.

Her strong loins fructified my strain in time;
With youthful charm, tender grace, and bridal
    dedication, she always did amaze.
Wax she gives life to foster our precious bond
    in its prime

By her natural wit, and tender loving ways.

I will be lured not from her suite, for more
 than the world's worth
Neither will break I the joy of our everlasting
 honeymoon days.
But, for the remaining breath of our holy
 matrimony on earth,
Bask I in the exaltation of our marriage,
 forever, always.

REFLECTION

Yea, straightened I the bend
Life has given me my fill
As come, I, to the end
Of my climb to the top of the hill.

The traverse of my generation's days 'ere
   simple and prose.
So tempestuous 'twas …laboriously I strive…
To sparkle the pearly bed of rose
In the persistence of keeping kindred alive.

Oh, it's wonderful…marvelous…to have been
   there;
To taste of the vintage life gone by.
And, now, that I am here,
I simply refuse to cry.

But, look I to the dying days ahead,
As my peevish bones' spirit rests
From the weariness of the life I led
'Till, I, from this earth, my maker divests.

THE PAST

Oh, resting spirit of ancient,
Grant me the privilege that the past I evoke
Bringing thee into the present…
Freeing me of today's miserably binding yoke.

Reverend, I know, is the relic of the sanctum of peaceful souls.
Nay, they shouldn't be disturbed nor desecrated.
But, o, the overflowing substance from my heart's dilating holes,
Inclined I to resurrect the holy species we have created.

From many metanoias, buried thee, I, into the void pit of oblivion;

Obliterated thine existence from my proud mind.
Alas, precipitated my once glorious spirit into the dark subterranean,
And upon a life endowed with doldrums, I now resigned.

And so, my dearly beloved resting spirit of ancient,
Grant me the privilege to disturb the beautiful past…
Bringing thee into the present.
So that yesterday's joyous and divine feelings will return, forever to last.

LET ME BE THERE

Oh, my love,
In the still of the night,
When the warm and tender zephyr
Rhythmically blows from thy slender nares,
Let me be there.

Let me be there
To use my right arm
As an arch about thy shoulders,
While my left hand
Deftly displays my covert inclinations;
As my heart,
My heart,
Beating its passionate…
Pulsating rhythms,
Tuned with the suggestive lines I whisper,

Exalt thine ears with euphony.

Oh, let me be there,
So that the warmth of thy svelte body
Joins union
With the glowing stimulation of my carnal being;
Filling me with desires…
Taking me higher
To the heavenly…
Glorious point
Where the rites of nocturnal passion ends.

Yeah, let me be there,
To use the esoteric arts
And induce the reservoir of torrid ecstasies…
Wild somatic fervor…
From their moment of respite,
From their torpidity
Into an uncontrollable spate…
A torrent of lovers' intimacy:
Flowing downhill
Through the vales
Across the meads
Quenching the drought of fiery pastures parched
Overflowing the rapturous slopes
Culminating into the abandoned waters

Of unalloyed pleasure
And enchanted satisfaction.
Oh, pearl of my heated soul,
I ardently implore thee,
Let me be there.

FORGIVENESS

Oh, my love,
Consider myself strong,
But now doeth I know,
I'm weak.
Fools in their obsessions
Accept not when they are wrong.
Behold, a wise man,
With dignity, his heart's desire
He'll diligently seek.

For, far beyond the threshold
Of a doxy's dwelling place,
I strayed to attain ephemeral aliment
For the carnal way.
And, like a ravenous beast,
Without tenderness, care, or grace,

I hurriedly preyed, and,
Hereupon, with speed, I set a pace
For the fulfillment of the doit that I did pay

And, now,
My guerdon to accept;
The consequences
I, now, to face –
There is no one else to blame,
For living the life of a blackguard,
Except for me,
I know.
For I,
Without compulsion,
Did lace
My heart and soul together
Under the besetting fleece
Of sorrow and woe

For there's an overbrimming pool at my feet,
From the effusive stream of my eyes,
Withal, my garb is soaked from rheum;
The engulfing darkness
Is causing me to slumber
In hibernation from lassitude.
I am conquered
By the million faces of doom;
I am but the shards of a broken coxcomb…

In purging myself of a selfish attitude

Yeah,
My Love,
A million scars
My heart and soul carry
From the carnal path
I did traverse.
Nay,
I am not in-need of an apothecary
As medicine is bootless
For the heart that is stained and perverse

My love,
There is one, and only one, cure:
To make amends,
My raiment I must tear;
And from my wicked ways,
I must turn forever away.
So, sackcloth and ashes I shall wear;
And to show my compunction,
My heart I must rend;
And look thee earnestly in thine eyes,
As forgiveness, I fervently pray.

For I'm resolute,
Never again will I be traitorous to you;
So, let this be the end of the war,

I beseech thee,
Accept my white rose of truce.
Pray, dwindle not thy love from me,
Away from my sphere, so far.
Decline not
My simple…peasant…
But earnest request.
Saying : It's over;
It's no use

Yeah,
My love,
I understand
Thy bitter resentment
Towards me,
Because I wantonly went astray.
Yeah,
My love,
I understand
Thy utter disdain
Towards me,
For my disloyalty
I caused love to disgrace.
But, this time,
In my heart,
There is only truth and honesty
So thee I'll ne'er again betray;
This time,

My heart,
Is accorded with what is right
So love I'll never again abase.

My love,
Thy broken and repentant
Picaroon
Invokes thy mercy…
Oh, I implore thee,
The purpose of my entreaty,
Don't thwart.
Yeah, discard me not
Into the dark abyss
Of the unremembered,
Like fading memories
Of the distant past.
Else my days,
Of the lengthening shadows
Of glorious paradise,
Will be numbered.
And the besetting life
Of confounding misery
And severe trials
Will perpetually last.
And, so, my love,
My everlasting love,
On my genuflected knees
Beg I readmittance into thy domain.

Nay, the folly of my repugnant act…
Of tasting the carnal way…
Will continue never.
Instead, everlasting peace, unmitigated love,
And heavenly happiness
Will undoubtedly reign
As we nurture our reawakening,
The fostering of our new life
In the rekindling of our union,
Forever.

HAPPINESS FROM A LOVE RESURRECTED

My love,
I am enlivened
Enthralled
Animated
And gleeful
To partake of thy resplendent…
Beauteous…
Smile,
Once again.

To know that the beauties,
Joys…
Rhapsody in ecstasy…
Of the past,
Are renascent…

Resurrected…
To be inthralled by the chain of love
Yet, feel, oh, so free.

Soul of my soul,
To be lost
In the twinkling of thine eyes
To savour the exquisite
Delicate
Wine of thy lips…
Feeling the warm security
Of thine embrace…
To feel loved,
By love;
And
By giving love to love,
Obliterated from my mind,
And soul,
The ache
The yearning
The gloom
The vacuum
And
The pain.
Filling the dark hole
Of my soul
With progressive delights.
Elating my nadir spirit

To the magnitude of cherub.

Yeah,
My perturbed
Perplexed
Life
Has been transformed
To one of unalloyed happiness
And
Euphoric joy.

Oh,
My love,
These moments
We no longer trod
The pugnacious zone
Of malignant living.
Instead, our gazing eyes,
At each other,
For each other,
Are the guiding light for each other
Along the path,
When the moon takes its respite.

Oh,
The feelings are of the magnitude
To fervently aspire
For a millennium years

Of a life time
So that the mere shadow
Of these memories
Elevate my heart
Likened to the rememberable grail
Of a blessed and wondrous tomorrow.

My royal flower,
To behold thee
At the break of dawn
Plucking the lilies
From the fields
Promenading through the park
In the young of the night
And being able to accompany
The surety of thy foot steps
With the uncertainty mine
Or
To savour the lingering warmth
Where thou just sat,
Vitalise me
With an unction of life…
Rubicund
And
Delight… happiness…
Every fibre of my soul
Bursting
With the substance

For existence.

Forsooth,
My beloved,
The wound's been healed,
The waxing gap's been waned
By the bridge
Of our resurrected love,
With the
Violently
Stormy days
Yielding
To the resplendent majesty
Of the everlasting sun shine.

UNDYING YOUTHFUL LOVE

Vernal hearts, your love you nurture,
By entrusting togetherness, all the way.
This be the sapiential motherly call of nature,
But, like wanton children, we did disobey.

Yeah, foolishly, from the spring of love, we did depart;
For we were young, simple, and weak,
With only temporal desires of the heart
So, foolishly, the sublunary, we did seek.

We wandered from place to place,
Yearning for the epicure comforts of our own.
But none we savour with charm or grace,
As, for moments of long ago, we continuously, in despair, moan.

Oh, there's this everlasting sentimental hold
On the memorably, glorious, past.
Albeit, now we be nigh of our days of old,
We still can make the early magical thrills last.

We give it only a try,
And the glory of youthful love we revive.
Nay, ne'er again will it go to rest, nor will it die;
Forever, its flames will be kept alive.

A DREAM OF SUGGESTIVE ADULTERY

Say, my Christian's heart is heavy laden,
With pure and unblemished insanity;
As the fairest of maiden
Gives unto the sun her virginity.

Seductively prostrating on her back,
With most glazen-like legs crossing ankle-wise
Struck I by a thunderous attack
From the sensuous gratification of my eyes.

With tender passion, they journeyed to her
    sumptuous breasts
To the soft, laniferous moss of her maiden
    hood.
Oh, wantonly thrilled was I, with so much

desire and zests,
I simply couldn't maintain the grounds I stood.

Yeah, I have to brave this precious chance.
So, reached out I for this creature, holy and great.
Lo and behold, tried as I may, I couldn't advance:
I laid unfulfilled…hooked to the tantalizing bait.

So, in frenzied desperation, tried I to shout
Even to utter a solemn oat'.
But, verily, no words came from my mout'
Everything stuck in my throat.

Then, suddenly, I was most confused,
I can never explain.
I felt an ear, with moist, being suffused
As someone hotly whispered my name.

Oh, heightened and mounting emotions flooded my life,
So, opened I mine eyes, in dismay, I to see
Not the morphine creature, but my loving and faithful wife
Emitting tender concern o'er what is happening to me.

THE ISLAND OF THE ISLES

How fair thou art, my love
As fair as the angels above.
Thy crimson lips are sweeter than all the honey
  comb of this earth.
Oh, thy laughter is filled with majestically
  sensational mirth.

Thine hair is as glistening, glossy like the
  wings of a raven
Thine eyes are of the colour of the blue heaven.
Thine eyes, my beloved, are as radiant as the
  stars above
The seductive motion of thy body is as graceful
  as a dove.

Thy smile is as blissful as the break of dawn in

spring
The warmth and freshness of thy breath filled me with zing.
The euphony of thy voice, my love, is the dreamy sound of a violin to my ears
Thy teeth are likened to the sparks of proud warriors' spears.

Thy skin is as smooth as an olive, void of the slightest mar
The majestic beauty of thine earlobes rivals the brightest star.
The mahogany, the cedar, the blue mahoe, aren't as fair as thee
Indeed, my beloved, thy multitude of pulchritude exceed the finest tree.

Oh, my love, thou art fairer than all the princely daughters of the earth
Little wonder every member of thy kind envy the day of thy birth.
Yea, thy beauty is so rare, precious…one of a kind
Every being privileged to breathe in thy presence, savour a blowing of the mind.

RESORT

Sail
Sailing home with you.
Sail
Sailing home with you.
Sail
After the year-long blue
My love,
sailing home with you.
Sail
After your work is through
You come home
To celebrate,
Me and you.
Together we dine
Sipping century old wine
With aged cane fire,

Where we be overpowered
By the imperious desire
Of nocturnal love.
Ecstatically
Tenderly…
Deliberating…
Savour the loveliness
Of thy body
All night through
Oh, sail
Sailing home with you.

OH

Oh, gentle rose,
Whose essence permeates the mighty breeze.
Oh, my warm and sumptuous lily
By the sweet crystalline waters.
Fluff thy blossoms about me
So that I be intoxicated with thy fragrance.
Open thy petals around me
So that I can shut out the cold.
Be my fountain of sugared juice
So that from thy petals, I get my fill.

Oh, reverential pearl of my heart,
Treasured preciousness
From the innermost seas
Bind me with thy love
Enchained me with the purity of thy being

Charm me with the blitheness of thy spirit.

Oh, my dignified…loyal…forget-me-not
Tender cherished flower of my soul
I beseech thy favour
When darkness seized my soul
When my body becomes prostrated
My heart be filled with sorrow
And my countenance
Pigments an ashen perspective.

Oh, fragmented marigold in all thy glory
Be the spring time of my morning
The autumn breeze of my evening.
Like fines of wine,
And the strongest of brew,
Under candle light
Elate my being
Beyond the threshold of supernatural control,
By the radiance of thy love
The warmth exuding from thy glowing hearth
And the passion of thy soul
Oh, now and forever more.

TWO HEARTS OF EQUAL LOVE

Tender is the rain
Drizzling in the breeze.
Gentle is the pain
From thy squeeze.

Beautiful are the flowers
Blooming at nights.
Soothing and exotic are the hours
When we are performing nature's rites.

Divinely joined, we two creatures,
Like the Myrtle tree and the turtle dove;
Richly endowed with the sublime features
Of twain hearts enchained by the bliss of love.

Hence to each other, we unreservedly reveal
The preciousness of nature's hiding place;
So that we can ecstatically expose the way we feel
When nature's bounty we, without shame, to grace

As we unashamedly get into the mood
At any moment in time
Where nature's bliss becomes our sole food
Upon nature's rapture we hungrily dine:

Untamed…freely…with ne'er a frown
Even, where, by the unprying eyes, we can be seen
You willingly let your gown,
Oh, so white and pristine,

To be deliberately unknotted at the bow
And becomes no longer clean;
As you, with unrestrained delight, vivaciously did allow
Your lovely gown to be stained green,

In fields, where grass tumbled
And weeds out of shape bent
Solid earth crumbled
And blowing flowers gave a new scent

In the tangled garden below
Where the more the shoots push
The harder the cockscombs grow
Into a wild and untrimmed bush

For the more the land is tilted
And the more water we pour
The more plants remained unwilted
All the way to the backdoor

From the path of our front porch along
And all of the outside of our domain
Feelings are very strong
So inside we came

Where, whilst not to be bested,
In our abode, here,
Everywhere we have tested
Devoid of any fear:

Our couches we humbled,
And the posts of our beds rent;
Over chairs we stumbled,
And, every day, our private chamber got a new dent

Yeah, tables are made for dining
And that much we have proved to be true;

Jamaica: The Overture of Caribbean Destination Passion & Seduction

The walls are worth climbing
And we have done that too.

The counters are well travelled
And benches need to be replaced;
Our rugs are ravelled
And the heat of the hearth our blaze displaced

And, so, betwixt the abroad green
And within our rapturous abode,
We have partaken in every scene
When through the bliss of life, we strode

And by the powers of valence
We coalesced across the gliding isles of nature
Culminating in free rhapsody's final musical cadence
With wooing words of unbridled love igniting the flames of rapture.

RETURN TO THE MOTHERLAND

I love thee with passion
I love thee with fire.
Thou art all my bounty of fashion
My humble heart's desire.

Oh, my feverish…blazing…love
Mine thou art for sure.
A glorious blessing from The One above;
Nay, I could never ask for more.

Thou art the soothing savour of my chagrin
    soul
The rock of fortitude in my moments of strife,
    always.
The warm…fervent…virgin in my days of ole
Yeah, the shining light of my sombre days.

Thou art the river of a generation
The one with whom procreation begins.
Thou art the land from which cometh a great nation
The blessed mother of great things.

Thy virtues rival the purity of a virgin
A perfect maiden among chastity.
The ointment that solace my spirit when it's raging
The evergreen essence of my life's entity.

Thou art king's food on a peasant's table…
The aureola…corona… of my lowly head.
The inspiration that makes life's turmoil more bearable;
The love that never ceased, even when lovers are dead.

Thou art a holy creation on earth
An angel without visible wings.
A blessing from the day of birth;
Thus, upon thy tender yet strong hands I cling.

With thee I'm desirous of spending the grey of my hair
The halo of my distant days…
Yea, the sole creature I want to be near

So that the fading embers of my soul will savour their dimming blaze.

AWAKENED PASSION

Part I the curtains of my repose
And behold my beloved in the arms
    Morpheus.
Oh, the vision of my nocturne beauty
So serene, angelic and sumptuous

Endowed my heart
With radiant sparks of purple fire
Inspired my Christian soul
With luxuriantly wild passion
And worldly desire.

Possessed by the magic of un-paralleled
    frenzy,
I desirously stretched forth my hands
To caress the aesthetic rose of regal splendour.

Ah, fluffed opened at once
The sparkling gates of beatific delights
To wondrous nature's fervor,

As the vivacious heat
Exuded from the burning fibre of my fair
    maiden
Carnal soul becometh I
In ravishing
The aged old mystical fruit of the Garden of
    Eden.

We zealously…deliberately…sipped of the
    stimulating…exciting…wine of
    enchantment.
Softly, tenderly, hotly…breathing words of
    endearment.

Reveled in mellowed pain
And overwhelming rapturous joy
Floating through the wild and abandoned
Of the blissful path of perpetual elation and
    content
Where twain souls entwine
In heightened glory
And convulsively thrown into a whirl pool
    gratifyingly spent.

UNTIMELY LOVE

One lingeringly attractive glance
And we hotly floated a dance.
We pleasurably dine
I am relishing wine
You are luxuriating champagne…
Seductively creating that suggestive flame.

We endearingly talk
Take a romantic walk
Gently holding hands,
As we skipped upon the sands
Of the enchanted beach
My unquenched lips yours reach

In a torrid kiss
Of nature's bliss…

Creating joyous emotional thrills
And the virginal cockle of my heart fills
With the electrifying urge
To coalesce and merge

Hearts twain
In an everlasting flame
Where it seems
Lovers rapture, and euphoric dreams…
Lovers paradise, and uttermost delight…
Are wondrously combine in one night

But we know
That this can't be so
For to him you have to go
And I to her, o,
To abide by the holy vow
Not to allow

Infidelity to take place
As loyalty we daren't disgrace
For loyalty is pure –
This is for sure –
And even though
There is no doubt that this we know

It is hard to see clear
When the heart sheds a tear

When the heart is in pain
When the heart has one aim:
To play the heart's game
That the heart knows is in vain

So the heart goes
But the heart knows
It must not stay
In the adulterous sphere where it went astray
The heart itself must retain
From the bourgeoning precipice of stain

And, this is true
For me and you
Things will never be the same
Hence, we'll whisper each other's name
In the deep, dark secret gorge of our hearts
Where the flow of tempting water starts.

ENJOYING NATURE

Behold,
It is the cool of the evening,
My beloved.
Come,
Put thy tender hand into the crooked of my
 elbow,
Oh, my dearest,
And let me walk you among the soughing
 willows of the valley…the sacred palms…
 the fine Blue Mahoe… the piquant cedars.

Yeah,
My love,
Let me walk you among the back bone of the
 beauty of nature:
The rose; the love bush; the lilies; the lignum

vitae; the poinciana; love-in-a-mist; the kiss
me over the garden; the lovelies bleeding;
the love-in-idleness; the dandelions; the
bugles; the orchids…

Oh,
My fairest bosom,
Let us stop for a moment.
Let us stop, observe and appreciate the beauty
  of the vegetation:
The green, green grass, the evergreen trees…
Yeah,
Let us savour the rich and costly rituals of
  nature:
The chirping sounds of the sparrows, the sweet
  songs of the nightingales…

We shan't stop here,
My dearest.
Let's proceed,
My fairest lamb,
Let us take a slow walk
And watch the brooks as they courageously
  fight their way through the cracks of rocks,
  between the gorges and roots of trees, and,
  after sacrifices…sedulous efforts… they
  gave themselves to the creeks…Oh, the
  creeks are no less selfless…they are flowing

into the rivers that are philanthropically
debouching themselves into the blue waters
below.

Pearl of my soul,
Let us take a moment brief
And appreciate the waters and its home for a while:
The slow, delicate movements of the microscopic waves; the glossy…reflective…surface. The silver grey of the whisp-like mist that hovers above the water.

Behold the ducks and coots
My love,
Aren't they beautiful?
The way they wade gracefully about in the water.
Look at the lilies and the water cress.
How they form an apple shape garden in the water.
Tenderly cared for, are they, by the gods' botanists?

How picturesque does the shore looks,
My love.
The godly erection of the lineary trees in the

background.
How majestically uniformed are the reeds and tamarisk.
Standing out in all their glory…in all their armoury…ready to protect their home from intrusion.
But, oh, my beloved, because of thy presence they are humbling themselves, lowering their swords,
With bowed heads and genuflected knees, they are bidding thee…imploring thee…to enter.

Oh, my beloved,
Come,
Take my hand,
And let me walk thee, with much deliberation, through the valley…through the mead…and savour the enjoyment of nature's beauty.

WHAT CAN I DO?

Under the shadows of the palm
Sitting in the park
From morning till dark
Waiting for my love
Sadly, sure,
I can't wait any more.

For it is nigh midnight
My mind contemplates your coming
But this is wrong
To have feelings so strong.
Feelings of a bleeding heart
And aching soul

With tears rolling from my eyes
I know you told me lies

Your many lovers
Craved for thy flesh
So, where art thou now?
With whom
Art thou,
My love,
Sharing thy warmth, during these hours?

I implore thee,
Depart and come unto me
Yeah, I have no riches,
No wealth
But the greatest thing my heart and soul give:
I'll love, cherish and adore thee,
As long as I live.

And so, my beloved,
Continue I to wait for thee
Under this mournful tree.
If ever thy lovers should put away thee
Don't hesitate
Please,
Don't wait
Yeah, come unto me
And forever,
Together
We shall be.

ONLY BUT A COWARD

Oh, love, 'tis too good to be true.
Far away, I'm not, for sure.
Yeah, I'm nearest to you;
For my humble abode is just next door.

Thy beauty and glamour behold I every day
The fragrance of thy body savour I in the breeze.
At nights the mind-eyes glowingly feast upon thy being, as in my bed I lay
But sentimental yearnings, my hungry soul they not appease

My feelings for thee, they only fuel
Setting my soul aglow.
So, locked I in a duel

Should fight I on, or simply let go

Of the glorious secret, yearning I to thee depart:
Telling of my adoration, love and profound care.
But soul of mine weakens…disobeying lips to the command of my aching heart
And the voice of the spirit of hurting past restrains me, when thou art near.

For thy power, oh love, is nary new
I have tasted thy poison and felt thy pain
So wary I must be o'er the things I do
Or suffer I the wounds of my soul again.

Howbeit, love, as our abodes adjoin each other
At the edge of our gardens, we might collide
Then we be strong enough to be weak enough to wreathe the beauties of twain gardens with one another
So that within one receptacle, sweet hearts may perennially reside.

LOYALTY

Love, the love thou so graciously given me
 others are trying to take away.
But, oh, love, I'm not bleared;
So, their seductive smile of illusion
I'm able to see
Their worldly hands on such preciousness, Oh,
 love,
They'll not lay.

Yea, they are arrayed in many illustrious
 colours;
Playing the crafty incognito game.
They'd arrive at varying hours
But, ah, oh, love, my answers would always be
 the same.

I unceasingly treat their advances
With the void of my interest
Cutting short their slimy glib…
Before started they, it's enough.
Know I, the stream from their mouth
To only satisfy their zest
Though their lines be sensuous and smooth,
Alas, I always rebuff.

For my fountain of grace, oh, love, nay vain;
Love's loyalty, oh, love, will never be
 compromised.
Love, you'll cover never thy face from shame
Nay, in men's eyes, oh, love, you'll ne'er be
 despised.

ECSTASY

In love,
I am
with thee,
oh, love.
Indeed,
a blessing
from the glories above.

Filled are my days
with picturesque scenes.
And,
Oh,
the dark hours
are lighted
with ecstatically
wanton dreams

Of twain souls
and bodies combine;
A holy spirituality
of feelings,
so divine.

Never
there's a night
devoid of sparks.
For the river of love
debouch
into the ecstatic ocean
Yielding bliss and joy
in one motion.

What else could ask I
Oh,
My tender lamb,
but to share all the rest
of my days
To partake
of the flaming splendour
of love, always.

THE BREAK OF SPRING

I'm excited and thrilled like an innocent child
Whose glorious days are about to start
Doing things, oh, so strange and wild.
I'm excited and thrilled like an innocent child
For the inclement weather is made mild
By the exotic love from within the embers of
Your heart
I'm excited and thrilled like an innocent child
Whose glorious days are about to start

FEARLESS PASSION

Oh, my love fairest
My love dearest
It's a wonderful, lovable night.
As the suggestive glim
Emits its late evening light

Let's convert worlds apart
Into a romantic throne
With rhapsody in ecstasy,
The world has ne'er known,
Like in the heavenly kingdom,
Where hearts and souls entwine
By a pure and unblemished love,
Forged by the divine

Out of the deep pit of passion fire

Where thirsts are quenched
By the body's gyre
That ignites the soul to rapture,
As the treasures tonight we share
Willingly and unhindered,
By the slightest speckle of fear:

From the distress of balance
From the nocturnal light's valance
From our own sanctimonious intentions
From society's solemn puritanical conventions

For in our connubial bed
All inhibitions and fears are shed
As we're empowered with the right to make
Our virginal beings consummate
The holy vows we take.

So, we ravish each other,
Like meat to an ensurient beast,
On this the night of our wedding feast
And when the morn breaks,
The world will see
A man and woman,
In happy harmony, be.

THE OVERTURES OF CARIBBEAN PASSION

Behold, it's a moon lit night,
My beloved.
Permit me to enter thy hospitable shores
And skip along thy myriad leagues
Of virginal white sands

Let my hands ripple the skin
Of thy blue waters;
Let my body rides by the motions of thy tides;
Let my head explores thy warm faunas below;
And let my being shivers in anticipatory blaze
Of excitement
From the strangeness of thy fulsome billows
Let my raft of bamboo enters therein
The head of thy dark waters, enjoy the gyre of

The ride to the pleasurable end,
Till the waters debouch at their warm
And welcoming embouchures to my advances

My exotic beauty,
I implore thee,
Grant unto me permission
To come into thy gardens

Within thy many gardens,
Oh, my beloved,
There are an abundance of glories
From which I'm desirous of having my fill.
Into thy gardens,
Let the physical language of my mouth
Raptures in battle:

Drink the milk and honey
That flow from thy lips;
Eat the nectar from thy lilies;
Sip of the strong and savoury potations
That saturate thy natural tongue;
Revel in thy glories
And be drunken by thy fermentations.

Allow me to sit in thy garden under the bushes
Of thy enamoured lignum vitae,
For the distillation of my body,

Oh, my maiden of mysteries
Yea, in thy gardens, let me sit,
My love,
And be imbued with thy warm embrace,
While savouring the comforts of thy habitation.

Oh, my welcoming maiden,
Aware am I of the millions yearning
For the warmth of thy comforting respite.
But, implore I thee,
Let me be numbered among the blessed…
Afford me the sublime privilege
To repose my head upon thy friendly,
Warm, and tender, yet firm, bosom.
Oh, how I yearn to feel the passion and glow
Exuding from the natural inhabitations
Of thy soul.

Oh, maiden of vitality, spirit, and life,
Grant me the privilege to be swayed
By the sounds of thy beats.
Let me be lost in euphony
From the melodious throbbing of thine heart.
Oh, let your melodies caress me
All over…
Feeling the joys of thine exotic abode,
As my feet measure to thy magical acoustics

My beloved,
I beg thee,
Let me be intoxicated
From the sweet rhythmical essence
Of thy being.
Oh, let the pulsating words
Of arousing passion…exotic words
Of warmth and comforts,
Strange words of tempting endearments…
Be the only sounds to my ears.

So that for all the days of my wassailing
Upon thy white…pristine…shores,
Thy many waters…
Let the world be jealous
From the ecstasy afforded me,
As revel I,
once again,
In the overtures of Caribbean passion.

FAREWELL TO LOVE

Oh, the blazing memories always
That will plague me for the rest of my days
To pore-on what I have done could
When at the chancel, I stood
Without knowing what to say
As I watched grief being poured away

My eyes, for my soul, did weep
My heart was sunken deep
Within the abyss of stygian, dark and gloom
My eyes saw the shadow of doom
For at the sole window's space
I beheld my beloved's face

Woebegone, despondent, and teary-eyed
When love has put aside…

When love has set free…
Its portion not meant to be
Then, the heart, love no longer owes
Pity, it's then love knows

That to show its true face
Ne'er happens in the first place
For 'tis always under mysterious clouds
That mock love shrouds
Intent on stealing your soul
But if you only remove mock love's stole

The face will reveal
The absence of what you feel
Tenebrous secretive eyes
Light the truth to the lies
That have captivated your heart
From the very start

'Tis from mock loves' slumber to awake
For love for love's sake
Is mock love, love, at last, sees
Love on its knees
Genuflecting slavishly to a broken heart
It's time from mock love to depart

Though you'll be crippled by pain
Surrender not to mock love again

For the same soft lips that kiss you to spell
Will be the un-parted lips to bid you farewell
For if anyone of mock love aught
It is ye who, in sables, descended the ghat

To the dark mountain base
And across the lifeless water space
To the tine of the triple spear
That cowers pirates in fear
Of the linear of corrupt corses
That overbrimming God's acre forces

The living to religious observations did awake
For the preservation of their soul sake
The disconsolate vessels that nigh in state lie
With an abundance of time a short go by
The white-gorget black- frock will shrive
To keep your soul alive

So that from a grief-stricken state ye
In the journey of time will see
That, thereunto, this side of the grave
Mock love is to deprave
The heart that love desires
And to conflate it into emotional quagmires

As thrice hearts, the eternal trigon to entwine
With chains of bitter suffering for the divine

For whose heart the holy troth is true
And, so, will seek no cause for the heart to rue
So, the feet will traverse not the path of a gant
Or be a cicisbeo, the body can't

But when by you, love is contemned
Like an aging cow, a lifetime you'll spend
Traversing at the back of the road
Where mock love mercilessly inflicts its goad
And for the folly of your ways
You will justly reap what mock love pays

A perfidious life and dread abound
For when you are not around
Mock love no longer sees your face
Only the one who is taking your place
And when ye is puissant, and thou art gaunt
Mock love knows it is time for you to avaunt

And this only provides fuel
For the most epic duel
That will inevitably start
For the heavier the shattered heart
The tauter to mock love is the gyve
And the deeper you dive

Heart first into hell
For you cannot break mock love's spell

As mock love has you under a malison
You would gladly imbibe poison
Though you're told poison kills, it is true
You would say nay; it is just a love brew

For you, for mock love, have a yen
But to mock love, you are merely a wen
As you stifle mock love for a filled space
You still trying to cling to your lost place
Feeling more and more eager to stay
But mock love wants you out of the way

For mock love has a new hope
So, on every tree, it sees a hanging rope
Mock love may think about it for awhile
Yet, that is not mock love's style
But, with a new hunger to appease
Mock love will give you the bane of Socrates

MY OWN INFLICTED PAIN

My love, it's my exceeding joy
That thou art in the comfort of thy royal bed
Savouring the beauty of thy
    tranquil…majestic… sleep.
Alas, my downcast spirit's reposing
Under the willows of the dead
Partaking of their sorrowful weep.

Oh, the moon's shining so seductive…so bright
The night is filled with a lovable glow
But the mood of my mood's not right
The receptacles of my heart with morbidity
    overflow.

The harness of my enfeebled back…
The waxing aches of my waning heart, cannot I

bear
Oh, my brine…tear-filled eyes…laid I not on
   thee for days.
Yeah, treated thee, I, with gross negligence, oh,
   direfully unfair;
'Tis no marvel; peregrinated us our separate
   ways.

Oh, if only could I impart my regrets;
Shedding my remorse;
Telling thee the depth of my care…
Earnestly adjure thy pardon;
Beseech thy favour once again.
But, oh, how far away thou art…
Thou art under the shelter of another abode
   somewhere.
So, resigned I under the soughing willows to
   the endurance of my own inflicted pain.

A BITTER LOSS

Yea, my soul doeth weep
My heart is heavy laden.
I'm at war with my sleep
Within the depths of hell my spirit's sunken.

What cruelty departing from this presence
Fate's dealt an unkind blow.
Oh, the agonizing pain from thy daily absence
No one will ever know.

Daily, feed, I, upon the vine of sorrow and woe
Drinking from the cup of a wretched mood.
With whom to share my life of nothingness, I
   not know
Hence, I'll always live in bitter solitude.

Yea, live, I, with the continuous flowing river
  of tears
Oh, darkness, loneliness, emptiness filled the
  days ahead.
Yeah, it will be a drudgery trudging the years
When life's a mockery not fit for the dead.

HURT

My body and mind are at strife
For I've lost the happiness of my wife.
Throughout this journey of life,

I'd ne'er been a drone
In the collective welding of our home
But now I am all alone

Enervated, despondent and sad…
Reminiscing on the glorious happiness I once had.
Oh, how could it be so bad?

After all these years
She no more cares
For this wailing creature in tears!

Tell me, why you'd to go
Thought I, our love was able to absorb any
 blow.
But now doeth I know

Love in its passionate game
Hinges on the precipice of pain.
If but its shadow was I able to tame,

Today, there'd be no strife
For I'd find another wife
To rekindle sparks in my life.

REGRET

Behold, stareth I at thy photograph,
With inward wrath
At the mocking vision of my life.
I'm reflecting on our unstraightened path,
With the yearn that,
Between us,
There weren't any strife.

But that we 'ere still together
Living happily
In one accord
Not untwined
One from the other,
With our beings scattered abroad.
I'm aware,
There's no rose void of thorn…

No love nought of jealousy, trials and woe.
But with thine empty space
A prolonged pain and morbid gloom's born…
A reclusive life in winter's set aglow.

Oh, my love,
What deeds wouldn't execute I
To have thee again…
Even to enfold thee
For a breathing moment in time.
A pack of wolves to the right,
A pride of lions to my left…
All I'd have slain
Or, for thy life, from the burning stake,
I'd gladly offer mine.

TREACHERY

They've cut short my life
The plant of my being they've uprooted.
They've embittered my spirit with strife
The treasure of my heart they've looted.

Like creeping shadows, they came in the dark
　of the nights,
Without making the faintest sound.
Yeah, put up I a great many fights,
Nay, destroyed not, I, their pleasure ground

Oh, it takes more than one ember to prolong
　the flame,
Hence, we be damned in the darkness.
Thus, the plunderers solitarily I not blame
For such acts of unfaithfulness.

I know my treasure has a hand
In its being opened to the greed of those
	thieves.
The way they understand
It's combination with such ease.

Indeed, it spreads its hinges for their lustful
	eyes
Allowing them to gluttonously have their fill.
Yeah, I realise,
Yet, seems I not to believe it still.

That a treasure once filled with gold
Is now unchaste and vacant.
It's no more a pearl to behold
But a filthy clout from sediment of wine decant

So much had I stored in that treasure
Ne'er had I thought anything could go wrong.
Alas, wretched am I…dispossessed of a
moment's pleasure
Tried, I may, but, o, I can no more be strong.

For they've cut short my life
The plant of my being they've uprooted.
They've embittered my spirit with strife
The treasure of my heart they've looted.

THE PRICE OF HAPPINESS

Take the sun shine out of my life
Shower my uncovered head with rain.
Torment my spirit with strife
Upon my back inflict cruel and vicious pain.

Like a beast of burden,
Let me journey through barren lands, wary
    hills…
Rugged mountains…to my days of jade.
O, make me a bed amongst mine enemies,
So that I sleep where they lay.
Put me at the forefront of the battle,
So that I be at the mercy of mine enemies'
    blade.
Yeah, cut my body into shreds,
O, beg, let my flesh becomes food for the beasts

of the forest every day.

Unto me, exact these things
I ardently implore.
Yea, do these things and I'll accept,
With great humility and pious consent.
Only beg I, deprive me not of love
Incline unto me the one I adore.
So that the remnant of my days, with joy,
Happiness, and exaltation of spirit will be
 spent.

A HEART INCAPABLE OF LOVE

They empty the recesses of their hearts in vain
And it's a picture of threnody to see them
   suffer in pain.
Oh, for their desires, I'm not game
They empty the recesses of their hearts in vain
I pity; they know not I'll ne'er be the same
I'm barren of the power to love again.
They empty the recesses of their hearts in vain
And it's a picture of threnody to see them
   suffer in pain.

MAKE NEW AGAIN

Behold, my love, here we are
We've reached the enchanted spot
Where lovers lay.
Let's sit, my beloved,
And recapture our abundance of glories
Even for another day.

Ah, they say angels exist
Only in the celestial abode above
But angel thou art
In the union of our love

With a narrow winding path,
Which ne'er always smooth;
But on the substance of our strength
We waxed in an ever-loving mood.

Yea, it's ancient knowledge…
A certitude of life…
Sparks of anger will always flare
Notwithstanding, the maturity of time is here

For us to enhance the waning light of our life
With recollection of our shining stars
Using the ointment from the substance of our love
To rid ourselves of our scars

Obliterating from our presence the omen of dark shadows
And start a new phase.
Happy living, unalloyed pleasure,
And complete togetherness always.

A WEEPING SOUL FOR THE LOVE LOST

Oh, comforting spirit of the dark deep
Take me in thy care and keep.
For my soul doeth weep
My aching heart cries
And the river of my eyes
With hail stones that ne'er melt
Viciously and mercilessly pelt
My enervated enfeebled healt'
Into the heather lands of doom
Where man breathes only gloom.

Oh, I know, I'm late
For the river of hate
Is in its spate

Overflowing its bank…
To the bottom my spirit sank
Ne'er to be consoled
Like the days of old
When my spirit moved like moths on the wold:
Free, worriless, and without strife…
Enjoying all the wonders, and beauties of life.

Now, oh spirit, here I am
Sea or land, without a gam
Humiliated like a lamb
Brought to the altar
Yet, not fit for the slaughter
So, pray I thee
Return the resplendence of love unto me
For my eyes to see
The glory of the fulgent sun shine
And out of this doldrum I'll climb.

NOTHING LIKE TRUE LOVE

Great riches and wealth
Man's privation they not void.
Neither does real happiness be felt
When love's cheap and alloyed.

When the divine beauty is admixture unchaste
    and untrue
Misery and pensive sadness perpetually reign
And mindful of what you do
You can't sooth the pain.

Unless awaken you to the simple fact
With derogatory love you dare not stay.
Thus, you turn your back
And wisely walk away

To the comforts of someone who loves and
 cares
Not your riches or power
But who'll imbibe your tears
In the brutally hurting hour.

MISERY

Behold, I've toiled and found
A fortune of immense worth
Yet, I'm mercilessly bound
In the greatest desolation on earth.

By the serpent's charm
Be I allured
Into the malignant storm
Of an incessantly tormenting sword.

Yea, gotten I caught
By a vicious and voracious vamp.
Pleaded I, and relentlessly fought,
Nay, there's simply no release from this fettering clamp.

O, what I wouldn't do to get away
Just to glimpse the sunshine again.
My drudged earned mountain of wealth I'd pay
Even myself, with courage, I'd have slain.

But I'm not brave
And my leeching serpent desires more than gold.
There's great inclination to see my grave
Long before the dawning of my days of old.

So, behold, our days dawn with bellicosity
And, throughout, enflamed with violence;
Our twilights pass in animosity
While our nights are slept in dudgeon and aversion intense.

ABOUT THE AUTHOR

TYRONE L. WHITE is a Jamaican who has seen, and experienced, the many faces of Jamaica – the good and the bad; the house on the hill and the shanty heading for the gully; the indoor-flush and the jakes; the safe and the brutality...the tourists' mirage and the Jamaica for the hustling Jamaicans. The author's writings are based on these experiences, as well as the belief that there is hope for the populace, provided that they recognise that there is no rigid taxonomy to life's journey, save that they, the people, being rational human animals, first have a duty to themselves to want a better life for themselves.

Made in the USA
Lexington, KY
23 February 2019